ANAKIN'S PODRACER

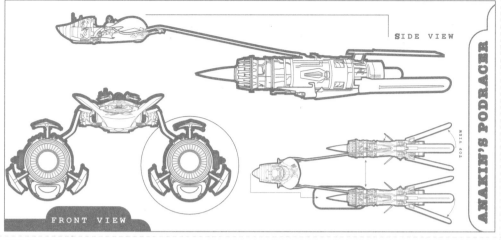

SIDE VIEW

FRONT VIEW

TOP VIEW

ANAKIN SKYWALKER

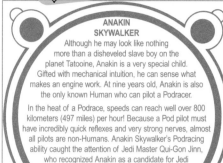

Although he may look like nothing more than a disheveled slave boy on the planet Tatooine, Anakin is a very special child. Gifted with mechanical intuition, he can sense what makes an engine work. At nine years old, Anakin is also the only known Human who can pilot a Podracer.

In the heat of a Podrace, speeds can reach well over 800 kilometers (497 miles) per hour! Because a Pod pilot must have incredibly quick reflexes and very strong nerves, almost all pilots are non-Humans. Anakin Skywalker's Podracing ability caught the attention of Jedi Master Qui-Gon Jinn, who recognized Anakin as a candidate for Jedi training. The Jedi-like reflexes required to race in the Mos Espa Podraces revealed Anakin's natural ability to connect well with the Force.

SEBULBA'S PODRACER

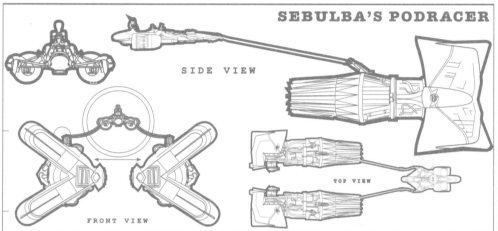

SIDE VIEW

FRONT VIEW

TOP VIEW

SEBULBA

An ugly Dug from the planet Malastare, Sebulba is the Pod pilot most favored to win at the Boonta Classic Podrace, held on Boonta Eve. Regarded as the most hazardous of all Podraces, the Boonta Classic attracts contestants from all over the galaxy. Most are wily opponents, but Sebulba's aggressive tactics and dirty tricks prove to be highly lethal to many of them. One secret weapon is the special "modification" Sebulba made to his unique split-X Pod engine—illegal flamethrowers. Such little "extras" prove quite useful to the Dug in frying unwary competitors!

NABOO STARFIGHTER

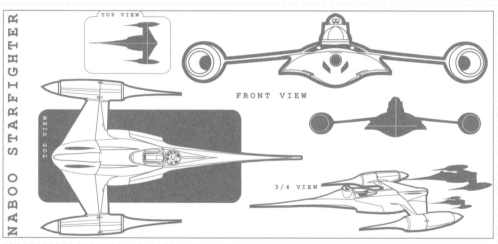

TOP VIEW

FRONT VIEW

TOP VIEW

3/4 VIEW

NABOO ROYAL N-1 STARFIGHTER

NABOO STARFIGHTER

Flown by the volunteer Naboo Royal Security Forces, this space fighter is a lightweight ship able to maneuver with speed and precision. Handcrafted by the Theed Palace Space Vessel Engineering Corps, each N-1 is armed with twin blaster cannons and ten proton torpedoes, and its pilot is aided by a galactic standard astromech droid, loaded through an underside hatch. A compact hyperdrive allows the spacecraft to fly in deep space. This is especially useful when the N-1 fighters serve as the Queen's Honor Guard on her visits to other planets. The N-1 is also used for planetary defense sorties, patrols, and formal diplomatic escort missions.

TRADE FEDERATION STARFIGHTER

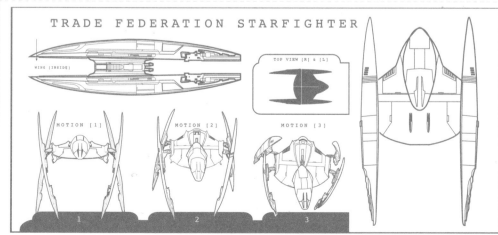

WING [INSIDE]

TOP VIEW [R] & [L]

MOTION [1]   MOTION [2]   MOTION [3]

1   2   3

TRADE FEDERATION DROID STARFIGHTER MODES OF OPERATION

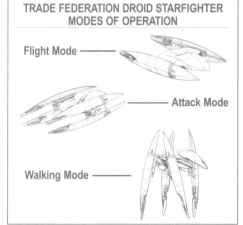

Flight Mode

Attack Mode

Walking Mode

STAR WARS
EPISODE I

ANAKIN SKYWALKER

MOS ESPA ARENA
PODRACING
ON TATOOINE

STAR WARS
EPISODE I

SEBULBA

STAR WARS
EPISODE I

PODRACE

STAR WARS
EPISODE I

NABOO
BRAVO SQUADRON

STAR WARS
EPISODE I

NABOO STARFIGHTER

STAR WARS
EPISODE I

TRADE FEDERATION
STARFIGHTER
TF

STAR WARS
EPISODE I

TRADE
FEDERATION
STARFIGHTER

STAR WARS
EPISODE I

Queen Amidala

ROYAL STARSHIP

JEDI vs. SITH

DARTH MAUL

JEDI COUNCIL

YODA

Obi-Wan Kenobi

"Anakin Skywalker,
meet Obi-Wan Kenobi . . ."
—Qui-Gon Jinn

ROYAL STARSHIP J-TYPE 327 NUBIAN

Handcrafted for the young monarch of the planet Naboo, the Queen's Royal Starship is a sleek and elegant vessel. This J-type ship is long and low, with swept-back wings and a 327 Nubian engine. The Queen uses her ship for diplomatic missions to other parts of the galaxy, including Coruscant, where the Galactic Senate meets. Because the Queen often has to travel to other star systems, the vessel is equipped with a hyperdrive. However, because the people of Naboo are peaceful, the Royal Starship carries no weapons. Its only defenses are deflector shields.

QUEEN AMIDALA
AND HER HANDMAIDENS

Brave, brilliant, and deeply committed to her people, Queen Amidala is the recently elected leader of Naboo. Ruling from the throne room of Theed's Royal Palace, the teenage monarch is determined to keep her planet and its peace-loving people safe. When the Trade Federation invades Naboo, it is her clever and courageous actions that help save it.

Queen Amidala's trusted confidantes are her handmaidens, Eirtaé, Sabé, Yané, Rabé, Saché, and Padmé, introduced as the Queen's most trusted handmaiden. Padmé shares a very special secret with the young monarch. When Amidala is threatened, these highly trained women are responsible for keeping their beloved Queen out of harm's way.

QUEEN'S CREST

DARTH MAUL

Darth Maul is a fierce warrior apprenticed to the Sith Lord Darth Sidious. Wielding a lethal double-bladed lightsaber, Maul is completely saturated with the evil of the dark side. His boldly tattooed face, horned skull, and glowing yellow eyes strike fear into the hearts of his opponents.

JEDI vs SITH

The ancient war between Jedi and Sith reflects a conflict between those who use the Force—an energy field generated by all living things—in opposing ways. The peace, serenity, and knowledge of the light side, utilized by Jedi, are countered by the anger and aggression of the dark side, adhered to by the Sith.

Those who are attuned to the Force and study it diligently can learn to manipulate its energy.

YODA

A senior Jedi of the twelve-member Jedi Council, the wise Yoda is highly respected throughout the galaxy and has been a Jedi Master of the highest order for over eight centuries. When he meets Anakin Skywalker, Yoda determines that the boy is too old to begin Jedi training. Years later, Yoda will express the very same thoughts about Anakin's son, Luke.

THE JEDI COUNCIL

The twelve members of the Jedi Council govern all matters concerning the Jedi. The current members are Yoda, Mace Windu, Ki-Adi-Mundi, Oppo Rancisis, Depa Billaba, Adi Gallia, Plo Koon, Eeth Koth, Even Piell, Yarael Poof, Saesee Tiin, and Yaddle. To enter Jedi training, one must be approved by the Jedi Council. As part of their training, young Jedi learn a philosophy known as the Jedi Code to prevent them from being drawn to the dark side of the Force.

THE JEDI CODE

Jedi are the guardians of peace in the galaxy.

Jedi use their powers to defend and to protect, never to attack others.

Jedi respect all life, in any form.

Jedi serve others rather than ruling over them, for the good of the galaxy.

Jedi seek to improve themselves through knowledge and training.

A FATEFUL MEETING

The passing down of knowledge from Jedi Master to apprentice has been the Jedi way for thousands of years. Strict training under a patient Jedi Master is what sharpens the natural abilities of a young Jedi apprentice, honing a fledgling Padawan learner into a full-fledged Knight who has gained not only incredible power but also the wisdom to know when and how to use it.

When Obi-Wan Kenobi finally moves from Padawan learner to Jedi Knight, he himself will become a mentor to young Anakin Skywalker and, decades later, to Anakin's son, Luke. The fateful first meeting of Obi-Wan and Anakin in the hold of Queen Amidala's Royal Starship is the beginning of a drama that will determine the fate of the entire galaxy.

OBI-WAN KENOBI

A Jedi apprentice, or Padawan learner, Obi-Wan Kenobi has nearly completed his training under Jedi Master Qui-Gon Jinn. While Obi-Wan possesses all the noble qualities required of a Jedi, he is also fairly headstrong and impatient. Nevertheless, his energetic spirit, loyalty to his Master, and clever resourcefulness show he has the makings of a great Jedi Knight.

Obi-Wan is equipped with a lightsaber built with his own hands—part of the Jedi training. Essentially a blade of pure energy, the lightsaber is capable of cutting through almost anything, except another lightsaber blade. These elegant and very effective weapons have been masterfully wielded by Jedi Knights for thousands of years.

STAR WARS®

EPISODE I
THE PHANTOM MENACE™

SCRAPBOOK

WRITTEN BY RYDER WINDHAM
INTERIOR DESIGN BY DAVID STEVENSON

PHOTO AND TEXT EDITING BY ALICE ALFONSI
ART DIRECTION BY SUSAN LOVELACE

ACKNOWLEDGMENTS

Sincerest thanks to the wonderful people at Lucas Licensing Ltd.
and Random House Children's Publishing for their work on this book.

At Lucas Licensing Ltd.:
Lucy Autrey Wilson, Director of Publishing
Jane Mason, Senior Editor
Iain Morris, Art Editor
Allan Kausch, Continuity Editor
Sarah Hines Stephens and Sue Rostoni

At Random House Children's Publishing:
Alice Alfonsi, Editorial Director
Georgia Morrissey, Art Director
Susan Lovelace, Assistant Art Director
and Kerry Milliron, Artie Bennett, Christopher Shea,
Irene Park, Fred Pagan, and Carol Naughton.

Movie poster image (page 3 and page 46, center)
courtesy Lucasfilm Marketing.

First Random House printing, 1999.

www.randomhouse.com/kids
www.starwars.com

Library of Congress Catalog Card Number: 98-83061
ISBN: 0-375-80008-5
Printed in the United States of America 10 9 8 7 6 5 4 3 2 1

Movie poster image courtesy Lucasfilm Marketing.

CONTENTS

EPISODE I

THE BEGINNING

Not so long ago in a galaxy we call home...

George Lucas created *Star Wars*.

When he began writing the screenplay about an interstellar adventure, Mr. Lucas realized it was too big for a single film. So he cut the entire story in half, but it was still too big, so he cut each half into three parts. He then had material for *six* movies.

Instead of launching his epic saga with Episode I, Mr. Lucas chose to begin with Episode IV, also known as *Star Wars: A New Hope* (released as *Star Wars* in 1977). The film introduced audiences to Luke Skywalker, a young man who hoped to become a Jedi Knight like his father. It was followed by Episode V *The Empire Strikes Back* (1980) and Episode VI *Return of the Jedi* (1983).

The original *Star Wars* trilogy made motion picture history, breaking box-office records and setting the standard for state-of-the-art visual effects. Years after their release, the films continue to enthrall millions of people the world over. Now George Lucas has given us a new *Star Wars* film.

Star Wars: Episode I *The Phantom Menace* takes viewers back to the beginning of this thrilling story, a time before the events of the first three films. While Episodes IV, V, and VI followed the adventures of Luke Skywalker, Episodes I, II, and III focus on Luke's father, Anakin, who will grow up to become Darth Vader.

In Episode I, the nine-year-old Anakin Skywalker lives as a slave on the desert planet Tatooine. It is while he is working in his master Watto's junk shop that destiny appears in the form of a Jedi Master named Qui-Gon Jinn.

On a dangerous mission to deliver Queen Amidala to the planet Coruscant, Qui-Gon is temporarily stranded on Tatooine. Soon after meeting Anakin, Qui-Gon realizes the boy is strong with the Force, and decides to do everything in his power to free Anakin and train him as a Jedi.

From the creation of C-3PO to the fall of the Galactic Senate, many secrets are revealed in *The Phantom Menace*. George Lucas believes Episodes I, II, and III will also make people change the way they think of Darth Vader. "When you actually get the whole story and see it in context," Mr. Lucas notes, "then you understand what Vader's side of the story is, what we have not heard yet, and it makes it a much more interesting drama."

So welcome once again to George Lucas's faraway galaxy.

Welcome to the beginning…

THE JEDI

Star Wars: Episode I *The Phantom Menace* takes us back in time, to the very beginnings of the conflict depicted in the first three *Star Wars* films. In *The Phantom Menace*, the Jedi Knights have not yet withstood the attacks that would decimate their numbers. They are still a thriving and vital part of the galaxy.

JEDI HISTORY AND TRAINING

Founded as a philosophical study group, the ancient Jedi spent centuries contemplating the mysterious energy field called the Force. After mastering it, they chose to use their skills for good, helping those in need.

For 25,000 years, the Jedi Knights served as peacemakers for the Galactic Republic. Operating out of the Judicial Department under the office of the Chancellor, the Jedi became the guardians of freedom and justice. They battled interplanetary criminals and settled cosmic disputes, becoming legendary throughout the galaxy.

Utilizing the Force, Jedi Knights can perform incredible feats of strength and speed. A Jedi's keen mind can see far-off places, project illusions, move objects, and hypnotize opponents.

Jedi are usually identified within the first six months of birth. At this early age, the infants begin their Jedi training. Because older children experience fear and anger, the Jedi believe it is unwise to train them in the ways of the Force. To enter Jedi training, one must be approved by the Jedi Council.

THE JEDI COUNCIL

Oppo Rancisis

Jedi Master from Thisspias with a brilliant military mind.

Even Piell

Jedi Master and Lannik warrior.

Ki-Adi-Mundi

The only Council member who is a Jedi Knight and not a Jedi Master. A Cerean, he has a binary brain that allows unique insight into the Force.

Saesee Tiin

Jedi Master and daring star pilot born on the moon Iktotch. Tiin is able to heighten his Force powers with the natural Iktotchi abilities of telepathy.

Adi Gallia

Jedi Master and the young and beautiful daughter of Corellian diplomats serving on Coruscant.

Yaddle

Jedi Master of the same species as Yoda. She is highly regarded for her wisdom, patience, and compassion.

Yarael Poof

Quermian Jedi Master legendary for his skills at mind trickery.

High above the metropolis of Galactic City on Coruscant stands the colossal pyramid known as the Jedi Temple. All matters concerning Jedi are governed by the twelve members of the Jedi Council.

Except for the Jedi Knight Ki-Adi-Mundi, all members of the Council are Jedi Masters. Although Qui-Gon Jinn is a Jedi Master, he prefers active duty to a seat on the Council. To become a Jedi Master, a Jedi must have successfully trained a young apprentice, known as a Padawan. To maintain balance with the Force, the Council does not permit Jedi Masters to train more than one Padawan at a time.

Yoda in the Jedi Council room.

Yoda

For over eight centuries, Yoda has been a Jedi Master of the highest order. A senior Jedi of the twelve-member Jedi Council, he holds a position equal in importance to Mace Windu's. The wise Yoda is highly respected throughout the galaxy. When he meets Anakin Skywalker, he determines that the boy is too old to begin Jedi training. Years later, Yoda will teach Anakin's son, Luke, the ways of the Force.

"Hard to see, the dark side is."
—Yoda

Mace Windu

Jedi Master and senior member of the Jedi Council, Mace is highly respected throughout the galaxy.

Plo Koon

Jedi Master and courageous fighter. Koon fought alongside Qui-Gon Jinn in many battles during the Hyperspace Wars.

Eeth Koth

Zabrak Jedi Master from Nar Shaddaa.

Depa Billaba

Jedi Master trained by Mace Windu, who rescued her at six months of age after her family was slain by space pirates.

Yoda and Luke Skywalker in *The Empire Strikes Back*.

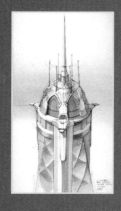

Production illustration for the Jedi Temple spire.

Production illustration for the Jedi Council chambers.

Obi-Wan Kenobi

A Jedi apprentice, or Padawan, Obi-Wan Kenobi has nearly completed his training under Qui-Gon Jinn. While he possesses all the noble qualities of a Jedi Knight, he is also fairly headstrong and impatient. Still young, he is energetic and quick to action.

Obi-Wan is a trustworthy companion, if naive at times. He greatly admires Qui-Gon and cares deeply for his mentor, but is often frustrated with the decisions he makes—including Qui-Gon's tendency to take other life forms under his wing. Obi-Wan is more inclined to follow the rules. He is quick to impress his Master, resourceful, and shows the makings of a great Jedi Knight.

Later in life, Obi-Wan Kenobi will himself become a mentor to Luke Skywalker, son of Anakin Skywalker.

An older Obi-Wan "Ben" Kenobi guides Anakin's son, Luke, in Episode IV *A New Hope*.

Obi-Wan and Qui-Gon converse on a balcony of the Jedi Temple in Coruscant.

Qui-Gon Jinn

Regarded as something of a maverick by the Jedi Council, the Jedi Master Qui-Gon Jinn is an experienced and powerful warrior. Noble, patient, and wise, Qui-Gon is closely attuned to the living Force, and his empathy for other living things is perhaps his greatest strength, even as it leads him to follow his own path. Qui-Gon is a source of leadership and knowledge for his headstrong apprentice, Obi-Wan Kenobi. Together, they make a formidable team.

It is Qui-Gon Jinn who travels to the remote planet of Tatooine, meets a young boy named Anakin Skywalker, and brings him to the Jedi Council for testing. It is Qui-Gon who sets in motion the destiny of the one who will bring about both the fall and the rebirth of the Jedi.

JEDI

Jedi Transport

Republic cruisers often serve as space transport for the Jedi. The Republic cruiser *Radiant VII* is an unarmed diplomatic vessel and is painted red to signal its diplomatic immunity. The planet Coruscant used the *Radiant VII* to send Jedi and ambassadors on many missions of peace throughout the galaxy. When the planet Naboo was blockaded by the Trade Federation, Supreme Chancellor Valorum dispatched the *Radiant VII* to the scene, hoping to avert a war.

Carrying Jedi Ambassadors Qui-Gon Jinn and Obi-Wan Kenobi, the *Radiant VII* approaches the blockaded planet Naboo. On the cockpit's viewscreen, the Trade Federation viceroy in charge of the blockade grants permission to board his battleship.

11

JEDI WEAPONS

LIGHTSABER

Essentially a blade of pure energy, the lightsaber is capable of cutting through almost anything—except another lightsaber blade. These elegant and very effective weapons have been masterfully wielded by Jedi Knights for thousands of years.

Part of Jedi Knight training includes the task of building a personal lightsaber. Although each lightsaber is unique, the weapon's basic design remains the same. The handle, twenty-four to thirty centimeters long, holds a power cell as well as one or more crystals—seldom more than three. The crystals focus the energy released by the power cell into a tight, bladelike beam. The blade's color depends on the nature of the jewel it springs from.

When a single jewel is placed in the lightsaber's handle, the blade length is fixed. But if more than one crystal is placed in the handle, the blade's length can be changed. By rotating a knob, the Jedi can adjust the focusing crystal activator, which changes the refraction pattern between the gems, resulting in a shorter or longer blade.

"The Force will guide us . . ."
—Qui-Gon Jinn

Blade Length Adjust

Blade Power Adjust

Focusing Crystal

Diatium Power Cell

Hand Grip

Belt Ring

Qui-Gon Jinn's lightsaber.

The Jedi are powerful opponents. Their natural abilities are sharpened through many years of strict training. Their minds are quick and they are often able to influence the weak-minded through special techniques. Jedi are also equipped with advanced survival and communications equipment, including their most dangerous weapon, the lightsaber.

Obi-Wan stands en garde with his lightsaber.

THE FORCE

Man-made weapons are not the true source of the Jedi's strength—the Jedi's greatest ally is the Force. The Force is an energy field generated by all living things. It surrounds and penetrates everything, binding the galaxy together. Those who are attuned to the Force and study it diligently can learn to manipulate its energy.

There are two sides of the Force: the peace, serenity, and knowledge of the light side and the fear, anger, and aggression of the dark side. Balancing life and death, love and hate, and creation and destruction, both sides of the Force are part of the natural order.

Knowledge of the Force gives power to the Jedi Knights. Its dark side empowers the Jedi's most dangerous foes, the Sith Lords.

Jedi Comlink
A communications device able to transmit and receive sound and technical readings.

Jedi Holoprojector
A hand-held projector able to reproduce ghostlike three-dimensional images called holograms.

George Lucas on the Force

"The Force evolved out of various developments of character and plot. I wanted a concept of religion based on the premise that there is a God and there is good and evil. I began to distill the essence of all religions into what I thought was a basic idea common to all religions and common to primitive thinking. I

wanted to develop something that was nondenominational but still had a kind of religious reality. I believe in God and I believe in right and wrong. I also believe that there are basic tenets which through history have developed into certainties, such as 'thou shalt not kill.' I don't want to hurt other people. 'Do unto others...' is the philosophy that permeates my work."

"Offhand, I'd say this mission is past the negotiation stage."
—Obi-Wan Kenobi

SAMURAI INSPIRATION

For the word *Jedi*, George Lucas was inspired by the Japanese *Jidai Geki*, which refers to a drama set in medieval Japan during the time of the samurai.

THE JEDI CODE

To prevent young Jedi from being drawn to the dark side of the Force, the Jedi teach a philosophy known as the Jedi Code:

Jedi are
the guardians of
peace in the galaxy.

Jedi use their powers to
defend and to protect,
never to attack others.

Jedi respect all life, in any form.

Jedi serve others rather than
ruling over them, for the good
of the galaxy.

Jedi seek to improve
themselves through
knowledge
and training.

Ever seeking knowledge and enlightenment, a Jedi never uses the Force to gain wealth or personal power. Because hatred, anger, fear, and aggression are made up of negative energy, Jedi apprentices are instructed to act only when they are at peace with the Force.

Jedi should seek nonviolent solutions to problems. Sometimes fighting is the only solution, but Jedi are encouraged to find alternatives.

Jedi cannot allow evil to occur by inaction. A Jedi must do anything possible to stop the forces of darkness.

MIDI-CHLORIANS

The Jedi have identified microscopic life forms that reside within all living cells, called midi-chlorians. These tiny life forms communicate with the Force and reveal its will. When one's mind is quiet, one can hear them speaking. A high midi-chlorian count indicates great potential as a Jedi.

SITH

Legends of the Sith go back thousands of years. A cult of renegade Jedi who gave in to the dark side of the Force, the Sith embraced the concept that power denied was power wasted. The cult was built in opposition to the Jedi. While the Jedi order was created to serve, the Sith only believed in domination.

Many of the original Sith destroyed each other and themselves with their own evil. The few surviving Sith were hunted down and killed by the Jedi. After the killings, only one Sith Master remained. To prevent future infighting between rival Sith apprentices, the Sith Master decided to take only a single apprentice. Thus, there were never more than two Sith Lords at one time.

For a millennium, the Sith maintained their order in secrecy, passing down their evil heritage. As they gained knowledge of the dark side of the Force, their powers increased with each generation. Nearly forgotten by the Republic, the Sith patiently waited for the day they would find a weakness in the Jedi.

Darth Sidious

Few inspire such an unsettling sense of dread as the robed, shadowy figure of Darth Sidious. A Dark Lord of the Sith, Darth Sidious ultimately plans to gain control of the Galactic Republic. Sensing the time is right for the Galactic Senate to fall, he quietly manipulates the Neimoidian Trade Federation into an illegal invasion of the peaceful planet Naboo.

Delivering his evil commands in calm, measured tones, Sidious communicates with Trade Federation officials by way of holographic transmissions from his quarters on Coruscant. However, when he discovers that two Jedi have helped Queen Amidala to escape his clutches, he takes a more active role and swiftly sends his dark apprentice, Darth Maul, to find and kill them.

"It is too late for them to stop us now . . . . The Republic will soon be in my control."
—Darth Sidious

Darth Maul

Apprentice to Darth Sidious, Darth Maul is a fierce warrior. His broadly tattooed face and his hairless skull, studded with a crown of short, hooked horns, strike fear into his opponents. Darth Maul wields a menacing double-bladed lightsaber. Soaked with the evil of the dark side, Maul's yellow-eyed ferocity is lethal when unleashed. With his double-bladed lightsaber, Maul can lay waste to multiple adversaries with fluid grace.

Sith Probe Droids

Sith "dark eye" probe droids are used for spying and scouting. Armed with many weapons and long-range sensors, these stealthy orbs can move swiftly across planet surfaces to track down almost any life form. Darth Maul uses Sith probe droids to locate Queen Amidala of Naboo and her Jedi protectors, Qui-Gon Jinn and Obi-Wan Kenobi.

Sith Infiltrator

This advanced armed Star Courier was customized in a secret laboratory and transformed into the Sith Infiltrator, the personal spacecraft of Darth Maul. The Infiltrator is equipped with many weapons and instruments of evil, including six laser cannons, spying and surveillance gear, interrogator droids, and Maul's speeder bike. The spacecraft's most incredible feature is its full-effect cloaking device, which makes the ship invisible and Darth Maul virtually unstoppable.

Sith Speeder

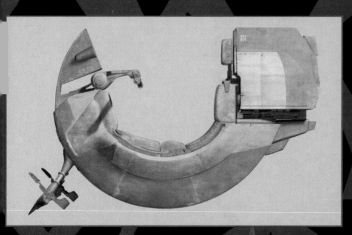

Although it has no weapons, sensors, or shields, the Sith Speeder is valued by Darth Maul for its swiftness. The speeder allows Maul to swoop down on foes and quickly attack with his lightsaber.

JEDI VS. SITH

The first battle between a Sith and a Jedi in over a thousand years takes place on the sands of Tatooine, just outside of Mos Espa. Sith apprentice Darth Maul, at the instruction of his Master, Darth Sidious, fiercely attacks Jedi Master Qui-Gon Jinn, who battles back and escapes. Although Qui-Gon reports the attack to the Jedi Council, its members remain skeptical that the Sith have truly returned.

Before long, Darth Maul closes in for his final battle against Qui-Gon and his apprentice, Obi-Wan. Lying in wait on Naboo, Darth Maul corners the two Jedi in the Theed hangar, and patterns in the Force converge. The Sith skills of Darth Maul prove more than adequate against the Jedi as lightsabers clash. Cloaks are cast aside and an epic confrontation takes place. Armed with a lightsaber igniting from both ends, Maul leads the two Jedi from the hangar, farther and farther into the Theed power generator. Leaping between catwalks and multiple levels and dodging walls of raw energy, they engage in an intense duel. As they reach the central core, it proves to be a day of destiny for all involved.

"At last we will reveal ourselves to the Jedi. At last we will have revenge."
—Darth Maul

THE TRADE

In a never-ending effort to increase its wealth and power, the Trade Federation uses battleships and droid armies to protect its profitable trade routes. Preferring to exploit outlying areas, away from the Republic's gaze, the Federation has recently targeted the planet Naboo. While it is illegal to invade a planet or challenge its sovereignty, the Federation has decided to escalate its blockade of Naboo, forcing it under the Federation's military rule. Was this shocking invasion an isolated incident or the first of more to come? Will other defenseless planets now fall victim to the Trade Federation's military tactics?

THE NEIMOIDIANS

Heading the Trade Federation, the Neimoidians are an intimidating presence with their mighty battleships. Cowardly creatures, they tend to exploit peaceful civilizations that have little power to fight back. Instead of risking Neimoidian lives, they deploy battle droids to intimidate the Trade Federation's unprepared victims.

EDERATION

Aboard one of their many battleships, the Neimoidian viceroy and his officers listen to the instructions of Darth Sidious via a holographic transmission.

"Our blockade is perfectly legal . . ."
—Nute Gunray

NUTE GUNRAY

The Neimoidian viceroy, Nute Gunray, appears to be in charge of the invasion of Naboo, but he is actually carrying out the transmitted orders of a mysterious Sith Lord.

"Have you ever encountered a Jedi Knight before, sir?"
—Rune Haako

RUNE HAAKO

An officer of the Trade Federation, Lieutenant Rune Haako is struck by fear when he realizes that the two ambassadors who have boarded their Federation battleship are really Jedi Knights.

TRADE FEDERATION INVASION TACTICS

When the Trade Federation blockades a planet such as the peaceful world of Naboo, it uses a vast array of powerful weapons, starting with the deployment of massive battleships into the target planet's orbit.

Trade Federation Battleship

Droid Starfighter Badges

TRADE FEDERATION DROID CONTROL SHIP

Massive antennae allow guidance of droid forces.

The Droid Control Ship is a specialized battleship that serves as the nerve center of the droid army. All Trade Federation droids are controlled by this heavily shielded "brain." As the Naboo discover, the best strategy to combat a Trade Federation invasion is to target the Droid Control Ship for destruction. The ship's heavily reinforced deflector shields make this a nearly impossible feat. Nevertheless, its destruction would cleverly cripple the Trade Federation's entire droid army in one swift stroke.

Flight Mode

Attack Mode

Walking Mode

TRADE FEDERATION DROID STARFIGHTER

These fighter craft are actually large droids. They are able to battle in deep space as well as in planetary atmospheres. In attack mode, the droids' sleek wings open to reveal hull-puncturing laser cannons. In walking mode, the wings reconfigure to allow the droid to walk on four legs. Stored in hanging positions from ceiling girders of Trade Federation battleships, droid starfighters resemble a colony of flying cave creatures. Each droid starfighter is indeed part of a collective, as the central Droid Control Ship computer is the actual "brain" that controls all the vessels. Droid starfighters are expensive to make, but their reputation as mindless killing machines strikes fear into defenseless populations.

TRADE FEDERATION DROID ARMY

Commander—yellow.

BATTLE DROIDS

Standing 1.91 meters (6'3") tall, battle droids serve as security, ground troops, and pilots of Trade Federation battleships. Receiving their instructions from a central source aboard the Federation Droid Control Ship, battle droids are incapable of independent thinking. Armed with blaster rifles and attacking in massive waves, they are lethal opponents in combat.

The number of battle droids remains difficult to verify, but there are more active battle droids than galactic leaders prefer to admit. Utterly heartless in the performance of their duties and obeying their orders with the steel-cold loyalty of machines, battle droids are instruments of destruction, feared by the more civilized peoples of the galaxy.

Standard troops—no special marking.

Security—maroon.

Battle droids with special duties are identified by colored markings.

STAP
(SINGLE TROOPER AERIAL PLATFORM)

The STAP is a small repulsorlift vehicle outfitted with two laser cannons. Extremely maneuverable, it is used by battle droids for patrol, reconnaissance, and combat.

DESTROYER DROIDS

Destroyer droids are deployed in wheel formation for swift positioning. After rolling into place, they quickly transform to an upright walking configuration for battle, becoming three-legged weapons platforms. Destroyer droids are armed with powerful laser guns. Unlike battle droids, they generate their own deflector shields. The Trade Federation uses destroyer droids both on its starships and on the battlefield.

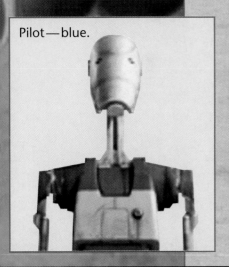

Pilot—blue.

Battle droids folded up for transport.

TRADE FEDERATION TRANSPORTS

TRADE FEDERATION MULTI TROOP TRANSPORT (MTT)

Carried within the landing ship, the Multi Troop Transport (MTT) is a hovering repulsorlift vehicle equipped with four blasters twin-mounted in ball turrets. Each of these large transports is designed to carry 112 battle droids into active combat zones. The MTT is heavily armored and is designed to ram through walls so that troops can then easily enter enemy buildings. Within the MTT, the battle droids are stored in folded positions on giant racks. The racks extend from the MTT to release the compressed droids, which then unfold to their combat stance.

TRADE FEDERATION LANDING SHIP

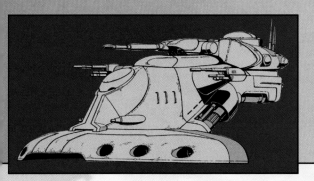

To transport thousands of droids, vehicles, and weapons from its battleships, the wealthy Trade Federation deploys C-9979 landing ships. The broad, H-shaped design of these transports allows great stability during rapid descents through planetary atmospheres. In addition to droid troops, a C-9979 typically carries 114 Armored Attack Tanks (AATs) and 11 Multi Troop Transports (MTTs). It can take up to forty-five minutes to deploy all the vehicles from within a fully loaded landing ship.

TRADE FEDERATION ARMORED ATTACK TANK (AAT)

Also carried within the landing ship, each Federation Armored Attack Tank carries a crew of four battle droids. In addition, each of these battle tanks has handholds on its outer shell to carry up to six more ground troops. Armed with six energy shell launchers and five laser guns, the AAT is deployed for the first time by the Federation during the invasion of Naboo.

THE NABOO

The small planet Naboo is located in a star system of the same name. Naboo is also the name for the humans who live on the planet. Although sparsely populated, the planet is home to two distinct advanced civilizations that have created beautiful cities—the Naboo, who live on the planet's surface, and the Gungans, amphibious beings who live in bubble cities under the planet's waters.

The large regions of Naboo that are devoid of inhabitants offer sweeping vistas and breathtaking scenery. The few cities of the Naboo people look as though they were constructed to enhance the natural beauty of the landscape.

The Naboo people are nonviolent. Their government is a democratic monarchy, ruled by an elected leader. Although the Naboo are peaceful, they do not have a particularly friendly relationship with the Gungans. Both civilizations misunderstand each other: the Naboo believe the Gungans view them as weaklings; in turn, the Gungans think the Naboo see them as a primitive species.

Aerial view of Theed.

WHERE ON EARTH IS NABOO?

Numerous scenes in Queen Amidala's palace were filmed at the Caserta Royal Palace in Italy. Asked why Caserta was chosen, George Lucas replied, "When we started to scout for locations we looked in various countries and cities, but Caserta was one of the most beautiful places on the planet and once we saw this, there was no question we wanted to shoot here."

The Queen's crest.

Queen Amidala

"I will not condone a course of action that will lead us to war . . . ."
—Queen Amidala

he recently elected leader of Naboo, Queen Amidala rules from the Royal Palace in the city of Theed. She is a brave and brilliant young woman who is deeply committed to her people.

he Queen moves with elegance, and her presence is enough to inspire even hardened individuals. She possesses not only grace, but the strength, wisdom, and courage of a great ruler. Her beauty is matched only by her determination—one should think carefully before crossing Amidala. She is extremely proud and will stop at nothing to keep her planet and people safe. When the Trade Federation invades her planet, it is her bold, defiant actions that help save it.

THE QUEEN and HER COURT

Theed Throne Room

The Queen's Royal Gowns

Escape from Naboo

Pre-Senate Appearance

Addressing the Galactic Senate

Post-Senate Appearance

Return to Naboo

Queen Amidala's royal gowns are artistic masterpieces, and the exotic wardrobe provides her with an air of regal mystery. Such richly detailed costumes have become a tradition for the elected royalty of Naboo. The teenage Amidala carries the tradition off with the grace, poise, and nobility expected of one in her position.

Victory Celebration

30

"We must not fail . . . .
Everything depends on it."
—Padmé

The Queen's Handmaidens

Queen Amidala's trusted confidantes, her handmaidens, know everything about their royal mistress. Whenever Amidala is threatened, these formidable women stand in between their Queen and danger. Their names are Eirtaé, Sabé, Yané, Rabé, and Saché.

Padmé Naberrie

Introduced as Queen Amidala's most trusted handmaiden, Padmé joins the Queen, Jar Jar Binks, and the two Jedi in their escape from Naboo. To protect Queen Amidala, Padmé and the Queen share a closely guarded secret.

Sio Bibble

Governor Sio Bibble is a member of the Naboo Governing Council, which aids Queen Amidala in her elected ruling position.

Although a peaceful people, the Naboo have a small armada of volunteers to defend them. "The Naboo Royal Security Forces" may sound impressive, but this modest service is far from prepared to defend Naboo against a massive planetary invasion. When the Trade Federation invades Naboo, the security forces are no match for them.

R2-D2

Property of the Royal Security Forces of Naboo, the astromech R2-D2 is one of several droids who serve on the Queen's Royal Starship. When the sleek vessel is attacked by the Trade Federation, R2-D2 proves himself to be both quick-minded and inventive. During his long lifetime, R2-D2 will gain a reputation for his adventurous nature. Although he's newer and less traveled, the brave little astromech appears very much as he will for many years to come.

Padmé prepares to clean off the battle-scarred R2-D2.

"GET ME R2-D2!"

George Lucas remembers working on his film *American Graffiti* with sound designer Walter Murch in the early 1970s. "Walter wanted to make some changes in one of the soundtracks. He needed the dialogue tracks for reel two and so he said, 'George, get me R2-D2,' meaning reel two, dialogue two, the second of several dialogue tracks. And I said, 'That's a great name, Walter!' and wrote it down in a notebook. When we finished work on *Graffiti*, I began writing *Star Wars*, but R2-D2 was still only a name. I wanted two robots in the film and wanted one to be sort of a human type, the other

Queen Amidala's Starship

The Queen's transport is a long and low J-type ship with swept-back wings. Powered by a 327 Nubian engine, this sleek and elegant vessel was handcrafted for the young monarch of the planet Naboo. In keeping with the peaceful nature of the Naboo people, the Queen's ship has no weapons, only deflector shields.

Ric Olié prepares for launch.

Ric Olié

A native of Naboo, Ric Olié pilots spacecraft for the Naboo Royal Security Forces. Piloting the Queen's unarmed Royal Starship, Olié helps Queen Amidala escape Naboo during the Trade Federation invasion.

Ric Olié's call sign during the space battle against the Trade Federation is Bravo Leader.

Captain Panaka

to be more of a computer type. I also wanted there to be humor in the fact that they were very different in temperament—one short and fat, the other tall and skinny. I don't know why, but from the start I thought of R2-D2 as being the smaller one, and then I had to think up a name compatible with R2-D2. After playing around with a lot of letter and number combinations, I came up with C-3PO."

Brave and resourceful, Captain Panaka is the head of Queen Amidala's Royal Security Forces. Often referred to as "the quickest eyes on Naboo," Captain Panaka is powerfully built and completely dedicated to the safety of his Queen. He never fails to catch the detail that might make the difference between success and failure in any security plan. Although he trained his forces to the best of their abilities, Panaka knows their number is no match for the Trade Federation's assault on their peaceful planet. In fact, he is only a captain because the Naboo Royal Security Forces are so small that there is no need for extensive rank organization.

THE SPACE BATTLE FOR NABOO

Badges of Bravo Squadron
and Naboo Starfighter.

NABOO STARFIGHTER

Bravo Squadron pilot.

Bravo Squadron vs. the Trade Federation

In a desperate action to escape the stranglehold of the Trade Federation, the Naboo Royal Security Forces launch the Bravo Squadron, led by veteran pilot Ric Olié.

Flying the graceful Naboo Royal N-1 starfighters into battle, the Bravo Squadron faces nearly impossible odds. They must confront scores of deadly Federation droid starfighters, as well as the armor and turbolasers of the massive Droid Control Ship perched high above the planet Naboo.

While the mission is daunting, help comes from a very unexpected place. A single Naboo starfighter—piloted by the very young Anakin Skywalker and the astromech droid R2-D2—is able to penetrate the Trade Federation's defenses. The starfighter fires two torpedoes within the massive Control Ship, producing a chain reaction that blows it up. With their nerve center gone, the Federation droid army is immobilized, and the tide of the battle turns.

THE NABOO ROYAL N-1 STARFIGHTER

This handcrafted, one-pilot space fighter is flown by the volunteer Naboo Royal Security Forces. Developed by the Theed Palace Space Vessel Engineering Corps, the sleek N-1 primarily serves as an honor guard for the Queen's Royal Starship. The N-1's chromium finish is purely decorative but is retained for tradition; only royal ships may bear the hand-finished royal chromium treatment. Also used for the purpose of planetary defense sorties, patrols, and formal diplomatic escort missions, the N-1 is a lightweight ship able to maneuver with quickness and precision. In accordance with the Naboo philosophy of harmony, the engines were modified for cleaner operation, which results in fewer atmospheric emissions during launch and landing cycles. Each N-1 is armed with twin blaster cannons and 10 proton torpedoes.

The N-1 pilot is assisted by a galactic standard astromech unit, loaded through a hatch in the underside of the ship. The cockpit is equipped with complete life support systems, while a compact hyperdrive provides the spacecraft with the ability to fly in deep space. This is especially useful when the N-1 fighters serve as the Queen's Honor Guard on her visits to other planets.

JAR JAR

Living in the vast underwater city of Otoh Gunga on the planet of Naboo, the Gungans are a race of amphibious beings. Led by Boss Nass and a ruling council, Gungans speak a distinct, fractured dialect that is sometimes confusing to outsiders. Instead of traveling over land in vehicles, Gungans use the massive four-legged fambaas and the nimble two-legged kaadu as mounts.

The Gungans are extremely intelligent beings. They have a strong respect for nature, and their technology is highly organic. In contrast to the peaceful Naboo people, who dwell in cities on the planet's surface, the Gungans have a longstanding warrior tradition. This is just one of the differences between the two cultures that have resulted in misunderstandings and deep-seated dislike between the Gungans and the Naboo.

From the Gungan point of view, the Naboo think too highly of themselves—or, as Boss Nass puts it: "Wesa no like da Naboo! Un dey no like uss-ens. Da Naboo tink day so smarty den uss-ens. Day tink day brains so big."

Gungan leader Boss Nass.

T H E   G U

An amphibious Gungan native of Naboo, Jar Jar Binks is an outcast from the underwater city Otoh Gunga. Jar Jar is very kind and helpful, but rather clumsy. It was an unfortunate accident with Boss Nass's *heyblibber* that caused him to be banished from his home city.

While Jar Jar often accidentally stumbles into danger, this sometimes works to his advantage. His honesty and knowledge of his homeworld prove to be a great help to Jedi Master Qui-Gon Jinn, who rescues Jar Jar during the Trade Federation's invasion of Naboo.

Owing a life debt to the Jedi Master, Jar Jar joins him on an adventure that takes him from the dangers of Naboo's core to the wonders of Coruscant, then back to his homeworld. There his clumsy yet brave stand with his fellow Gungans against the Federation's droid army raises him in the eyes of his tribe from scorned outcast to beloved hero.

Jar Jar's favorite saying: "How wude!"

"Why mesa always da one?"
—Jar Jar Binks

Bongo

Used by the Gungans for underwater transport, the bongo is a small, efficient submarine. Because the Gungans prefer to create things that are in harmony with nature, the bongo's hull is organically grown. Even its shape blends in perfectly with the undersea world, resembling the planet's sea life. Unfortunately, this design also makes the bongo appear to be a very tasty morsel to the giant sea creatures that live in Naboo's dangerous core. Although the bongo's hull is sturdy, it is not quite sturdy enough to withstand the bite of the opee sea killer, sando aqua monster, or colo claw fish—which is why trips through the core are seldom undertaken!

N G A N S

GUNGAN

Gungans have a strong warrior tradition and are always ready for battle. However, while they never hesitate to defend themselves, they rarely start fights.

Gungan warriors meet their enemy with a variety of organic, creature-borne weaponry. Harnessing energy from the depths of their planet, they produce plasma covered energy balls that are thrown with mallets. Their powerful shield generators produce protective shields that are capable of withstanding laser fire and other projectiles. It is a mistake to underestimate the power of the cunning Gungans!

Kaadu

Gungans have a close bond with the kaadu, who serve as trusted mounts in both peacetime and combat. These two-legged swamp runners have strong legs, great endurance, and keen senses of smell and hearing. They are powerful and loyal creatures and are beloved by their Gungan masters.

Fambaa

Notorious for their small brains, fambaas are large, sluggish, four-legged Naboo swamp lizards. Despite their slow response to the commands of their Gungan masters, the fambaas are valued for their unflappable steadfastness in the face of enemy fire. Their thick, scaly hides even provide a natural armor.

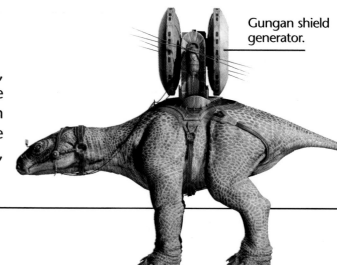

Gungan shield generator.

Gungan Shield Generator

Used to protect warriors from enemy fire, the Gungan shield generator produces a bubble-like energy field. When several of these shield generators are linked together, they form an energy umbrella that can protect the entire Gungan army. These large devices are mounted on the backs of fambaas for transport into battle.

WARRIORS

THE LAND BATTLE FOR NABOO
Gungans vs. Trade Federation

Rising on their kaadu from the misty swamps, the Gungan army assembles to wage a last stand against the Trade Federation's invading droid army on the grassy plains of Naboo.

The Gungan forces, led by General Ceel, have brought all of their organic resources: powerful energy balls, cestas, and massive shield generators, which they hope will protect them from the Trade Federation artillery.

The Trade Federation army, led by droid ground commander OOM-9, proves to be a formidable opponent. Armored attack tanks, flying STAPs, large transports, and battalions of battle and destroyer droids make for a deadly contrast to the native Gungan forces. The only chance the Gungans have is to hold out against the droid army until the space battle, taking place high above Naboo, destroys the Trade Federation's orbiting Droid Control Ship, which will stop the droid army in its tracks.

The Gungan electropole has an electric charge at the end of the pole that can frighten off dangerous sea life or stun unwanted intruders. In battle, electropoles can be thrown like spears.

The Gungan mallet and mallet pole are used by warriors in battle to throw energy balls at opponents. The mallet is a short single-handed device. The mallet pole, also known as a cesta, has a cup on one end and can also be used in hand-to-hand combat like a quarterstaff.

Ground commander OOM-9.

Gungan warrior Captain Tarpals prepares to follow General Ceel into battle.

CREATURES OF THE CORE

Opee Sea Killer

A vicious, multi-legged crustacean, the opee sea killer lives in the ocean depths of Naboo. Lashing out and snagging victims with its adhesive tongue, the opee then draws its captured meal into its sharp-toothed maw.

Colo Claw Fish

Dwelling in hidden tunnels along the oceanic floor of Naboo, the spine-studded colo claw fish can lie still for hours, ever ready to move fast and snare its prey within its powerful hooked claws.

The colo's turquoise trimmings are fluorescent; they glow in the dark water depths where the colo lives.

Veiled in dark mystery, the deepest waters of Naboo are the stuff of nightmares. Filled with monstrous—and hungry—sea creatures, the "core" is regarded as a watery deathtrap. Traveling through the terrifying murk at the center of the planet may be the speediest way to traverse Naboo's waters, but it is also the most dangerous.

Sando Aqua Monster

A snake-bodied leviathan with immense snapping jaws, Naboo's sando aqua monster is constantly eating to maintain its gargantuan form. Easily inhaling entire schools of fish, the sando is ever searching for larger meals.

TATOOINE

Located in the Outer Rim Territories of space, the desert planet Tatooine orbits two suns, the binary stars known as Tatoo I and Tatoo II. Years before the birth of Anakin Skywalker, mining colonies searched Tatooine for precious minerals and ores. Finding nothing of value, many colonists fled the planet. Their abandoned mining equipment and machinery were claimed by the Jawas, dwarfish natives of Tatooine. According to Jawa folklore, the great Tatooine desert known as the Dune Sea was once a true ocean. Ancient fossil-bearing rock and eroded canyons seem to confirm the Jawas' stories, but most people find it impossible to believe water ever flowed on the planet's arid, sand-covered surface.

Like the Jawas, Tusken Raiders are natives of Tatooine. Also known as Sand People, they are nomadic and ride unusually thick-furred banthas. Sand People and Jawas wear heavy robes to protect themselves from the heat of Tatooine's suns. Unlike the Jawas, Sand People are fierce fighters who dislike technology and humans.

Because Tatooine is far beyond the reach of the Galactic Republic and the Trade Federation, it is a popular destination for smugglers, criminals, and exiles. The crime-loving Hutts control Tatooine's economy, and most businesses there won't accept Republic credits.

WHERE ON EARTH IS TATOOINE?

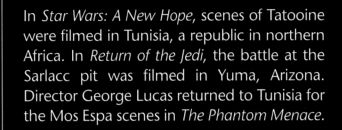

In *Star Wars: A New Hope*, scenes of Tatooine were filmed in Tunisia, a republic in northern Africa. In *Return of the Jedi*, the battle at the Sarlacc pit was filmed in Yuma, Arizona. Director George Lucas returned to Tunisia for the Mos Espa scenes in *The Phantom Menace*.

Jawas, dwarfish natives of Tatooine.

Tusken Raiders, also known as Sand People, dress to protect themselves from the harsh environment of their home planet.

MOS ESPA

A Mos Espa merchant.

Anakin, Qui-Gon, and Padmé stop by Jira's fruit stand.

Jar Jar snags a sample from a food stall.

Down a shallow canyon called the Xelric Draw, just on the lip of the Dune Sea, lies the sprawling city of Mos Espa. From above, the city looks like a gnarled serpent, hugging the sand to escape the heat. The buildings are mostly thick-walled domes, curved as a defense against the twin suns. The streets are wide and bordered by many shops and stalls.

Mos Espa is also a bustling spaceport. Because neither the Galactic Republic nor the Trade Federation has any jurisdiction over Tatooine, many aliens believe they avoid paying high tariffs by doing business in Mos Espa. But since the Tatooine system is controlled by the devious Hutts, few travelers actually save money when visiting Mos Espa. Attracted by inexpensive hotels and cantinas, salesmen and tourists soon find themselves in the Hutts' casinos and gambling dens, losing their profits at the chance cube tables.

Always interested in any sport on which they can wager, the Hutts also organize the Mos Espa Podraces.

Many traders pass through the Mos Espa marketplace.

Qui-Gon Jinn bargains with Watto outside his junk shop.

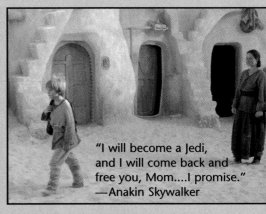

"I will become a Jedi, and I will come back and free you, Mom....I promise."
—Anakin Skywalker

ANAKIN SKYWALKER

A disheveled nine-year-old with blue eyes, Anakin Skywalker is earnest, hardworking, and always ready to help those in need. Though he is a slave owned by the trader Watto on Tatooine, young Anakin's quick reflexes have gained him a reputation as the only Human in Mos Espa who can pilot a Podracer.

Anakin may look like a normal boy, but he is very special and gifted. A natural mechanic, Anakin has keen intuition with electronic equipment and seems to sense what repairs an engine might need. Never far from a set of tools, he has secretly built his own custom Pod and is skilled at building droids, too.

Anakin is also incredibly strong with the Force, although he has never been made aware of his potential. Living in humble slave quarters, he longs to become a star pilot and experience a world of adventure.

Hopeful, optimistic, and good-hearted, Anakin dreams of gaining his freedom and training to become a Jedi. After meeting the Jedi Master Qui-Gon Jinn, both of his wishes come true. But once his freedom is won, it is Obi-Wan, not Qui-Gon, who becomes his mentor.

Although Anakin does not yet know it, his destiny will shape the fate of the galaxy.

Shmi Skywalker bidding farewell to Anakin.

SHMI SKYWALKER

Also enslaved by Watto, Anakin's mother, Shmi Skywalker, is a kind and brave woman who has instilled in her son a thoughtful nature. Although she dreads the possibility of losing her son, she knows he is special and will face a brighter future if he leaves Tatooine.

"The biggest problem in the universe is that no one helps each other." —**Shmi Skywalker**

WATTO THE TOYDARIAN

Watto is a junk dealer in Mos Espa. A Toydarian, Watto has a sharp mind for business and is not easily tricked. Watto is also a gambler and counts the slaves Shmi and Anakin Skywalker among his winnings from Gardulla the Hutt.

"I'm a Toydarian. Mind tricks don't work on me—only money!" —**Watto**

Shmi Skywalker in her home on Tatooine.

C-3PO

Using scrap metal and spare parts, Anakin Skywalker builds an experimental protocol droid on Tatooine. Naming the droid C-3PO, Anakin hopes the droid will help his mother around their home.

Still under construction, C-3PO requires a lot of metal plating before he'll be considered a proper protocol droid. If he knew the risks and dangers that await him, the skittish C-3PO might want to remain unfinished.

Mos Espa is one of the few places in the galaxy that allow the dangerous sport of Podracing. A high-speed, adrenaline-packed contest, Podracing is a favorite spectator pastime for many Tatooine residents. For participants, however, the races bring intense competition and danger. With combustible engines tearing over rocky terrain at high speeds, many racers crash and burn in a single competition. The Mos Espa course itself is the most dangerous of all courses, with terrifying drops and tortuous curves. At Jag Crag Gorge, racers must negotiate a twisting channel, then scream across high flats. At Metta Drop, they must pull out of the plunge and level out before nose-diving into the rocks below. Contestants are even subject to potshots by sniping Tusken Raiders. Yet for those who emerge victorious, fame and fortune await!

PODRACERS

A Pod is a small cockpit pulled by two high-powered engines. Energy binders lock the engines to each other, and steelton control cables connect the engines to the Pod. Seated within the cockpit, a Pod pilot operates thruster bars, which control power to the engines.

In the heat of a race, speeds can reach well over 800 kilometers (497 miles) per hour! Because a Pod pilot must have incredibly quick reflexes and very strong nerves, almost all pilots are non-Humans. Anakin Skywalker is the only known Human Podracer.

Since alien pilots differ greatly in shape, size, and weight, the Pods are heavily customized to match the demands of the individual pilots.

TATOOINE PODRACES

From his personal box at the Mos Espa Arena, the vile gangster Jabba the Hutt hosts the Boonta Eve Race. In the future, Jabba will become an increasingly powerful figure in the criminal underworld.

Tusken Raiders are one of the many dangerous obstacles Pod pilots must avoid.

Anakin Skywalker's Podracer

SEBULBA

A Dug from Malastare who drives a distinctive split-X Podracer. It is said that in all of Mos Espa, there is no better Pod pilot than Sebulba. This aggressive alien will stop at nothing to win a race. He uses dirty racer's tricks and adds certain illegal "modifications" to his high-performance Pod—for example, flamethrowers are mounted on his split-X engine, ready to cook unwary competitors! The only thing that delights the self-centered and self-indulgent Sebulba more than winning a Podrace is watching the demise of another racer.

Teemto Pagalies

A Veknoid outcast with the longest pair of Podrace engines in the Boonta Eve Race.

BOONTA EVE RACE
(a.k.a. BOONTA CLASSIC)
PODRACE CONTESTANTS

The Boonta Eve Race is one of the biggest Podraces on Tatooine. Contestants come from all over the galaxy to compete in this grueling event. Here are some of the starting pilots:

Anakin Skywalker

A nine-year-old Human boy who has competed in more than half a dozen Podraces, but has yet to finish even *one*. Although far from a favorite at the Boonta Classic, Anakin is determined not only to finish but also to beat his rival, Sebulba, and win. Anakin enjoys the distinction of being the only Human in Mos Espa who is able to race Pods. It is this unique ability that catches the attention of Jedi Master Qui-Gon Jinn. Any Human boy who can race Pods must possess Jedi-like reflexes—and, therefore, might be considered as a candidate for Jedi training.

Mawhonic

A triple-eyed Podracer who crashes his Pod into a large rock formation when Sebulba forces him off the course in the first lap.

Gasgano

A twenty-four-fingered Xexto and a popular favorite in the Boonta Eve Race.

Ben Quadinaros

A Toong whose hastily rented Podracer never makes it past the starting line.

Ody Mandrell

A native of Tatooine who has an appetite for high-speed thrills.

DROIDS

Droids are used all over the galaxy to perform specific and often difficult tasks. Although these mechanical beings are generally equipped with some level of artificial intelligence, they are often treated as property or slaves by their creators.

Droids communicate via a program language that most organic creatures can't understand. Only droids who must regularly interact with organic beings are provided with speech synthesizers. Even on an Outer Rim planet like Tatooine, where slavery is legal, there is still a use for droids. In Mos Espa, specialized droids are used in the sport of Podracing.

PIT DROIDS

Pit droids are programmed to be technicians that make quick, basic repairs. They are used as crew members by Tatooine Podracers. Able to lift many times their own weight, pit droids are highly durable and are designed to fold up to compact size when given a swift hit on the nose. Unfortunately, pit droids also have a habit of getting underfoot. They tend to bicker with one another and get into unpredictable mischief.

CAM DROIDS

Cam droids are robot cameras used to great effect during Podraces. Able to follow the exciting high-speed racing action across the vast course, the cam droids send pictures back to the viewing platforms, where spectators watch the race on viewscreens.

PROTOCOL DROIDS

Often used as diplomatic aides and translators, protocol droids are programmed to communicate in many languages. They are considered something of a luxury and are usually owned by high-level individuals.

TC-3, the Neimoidians' protocol droid, is used to greet and serve visiting dignitaries.

ASTROMECH DROIDS

Specializing in starship maintenance and repair, astromech droids also assist with piloting and navigation. They come in a variety of models, and are used by many starfaring civilizations.

Because of its extensive sensor package and variety of tools, the R2 unit is especially popular. These units can operate in deep space, interfacing with fighter craft and computer systems to augment the capabilities of ships and their pilots, usually from a socket behind the cockpit. R2s monitor and diagnose problems with flight performance, map and store hyperspace data, and pinpoint technical errors.

These meter-high droids have two treaded legs to provide mobility and a third leg that can drop down for extra stability on rough terrain. Astromechs also have flotation devices and a periscoping visual scanner that can guide them while they are submerged.

GNK ("GONK") POWER DROID

These boxy droids are practically walking batteries. Their job is to provide power to other droids and machinery. When power droids are working, they make a funny guttural noise that sounds like a "gonk, gonk," which is how they received their nickname.

C O R U

On nearly every astrogation chart in the galaxy, the coordinates for Coruscant are set at zero-zero-zero—the center. For tens of thousands of years, Coruscant has been the center of power and authority, a world rich in history and culture. The entire surface of Coruscant is covered by a sprawling cityscape several kilometers deep. Billions of people live in the multi-level structures, with the wealthiest citizens enjoying the uppermost luxury suites.

The capital of Coruscant is Galactic City. Drawing people from far across interstellar space, this city serves as the permanent headquarters of the Galactic Senate. Galactic City is also home to an order of even greater power: the Jedi Council.

Coruscant skyline—Day.

Coruscant skyline—Sunset.

Coruscant skyline—Evening.

WHERE ON EARTH IS CORUSCANT?

Unlike the other worlds in *The Phantom Menace*, Coruscant did not use any already-existing locations on Earth. The look of this astonishing city-planet got its start when Director George Lucas described his vision of the planet to artist Ralph McQuarrie, the Concept Designer for the first *Star Wars* trilogy. McQuarrie created several striking paintings of the planet, with pyramid-shaped towers looming miles above Coruscant's skyscraper-covered surface. Later, when work began on Episode I, Lucas encouraged Concept Designer Doug Chiang to create new production drawings for Coruscant. Chiang said, "George told me he wanted something as fresh as Ralph's original work, but different. He wanted Coruscant to be a city of mixtures…a combination of really sleek architecture with some older-style architecture. It was like taking Manhattan and scaling it way, way up. All of these buildings are mile- and two-mile-high skyscrapers. We never really see the floor, because this is a city of such large buildings. Each one of them is several blocks wide at the base." Coruscant's realistic cityscapes were constructed on computers, and the live-action scenes were filmed at Leavesden Studios in England. The result is a world unlike any other.

THE GALACTIC SENATE

Uniting representatives from many star systems, the Senate is made up of Human and alien dignitaries. All member worlds in the galaxy elect these politicians to serve as their representatives. The Senate creates laws, pacts, and treaties, and it governs the galactic union of planets and star systems known as the Republic. The Senate is led by a Supreme Chancellor, who is elected to the position by his fellow Senators to serve as roving ambassador, arbiter, policymaker, and planner.

The Senators work in the Galactic Senate Building, a large, distinctive domed building that stands out, even against the grand cityscape of Coruscant. Within the Senate Building is an immense circular assembly area called the Senate Chamber. This is where thousands of Senators and their aides meet.

Queen Amidala moves to address the Galactic Senate.

"I was not elected to watch my people suffer and die while you discuss this invasion in a committee . . ."
—Queen Amidala

Senate congressional boxes are floating platforms that allow Senators and visiting dignitaries to move to the center of the Senate floor and address the entire chamber.

A Rodian Senator.

Chancellor Valorum and his aides.

Senator Palpatine of Naboo.

SENATOR LOTT DOD

The Senator for the Trade Federation, Lott Dod is usually seen in the company of Trade Federation barons, who control the profitable trade routes in outlying star systems. Many members of the Senate dispute the legality of the Federation's methods—such as the blockade of the peaceful planet Naboo. But Dod is determined to defend the Trade Federation from his congressional box in the Senate Chamber and see that the greedy interests of the barons remain protected.

SENATOR PALPATINE

A sector Senator representing the planet Naboo as well as hundreds of other star systems, Palpatine has seemed to lack any real ambition for many years. However, with the growing corruption in and around the Republic, Palpatine sees a way to gain power. When the right moment comes, he convinces the Queen of Naboo to call for a vote of no confidence against the Senate's sitting Supreme Chancellor, Valorum. The resulting vote places Senator Palpatine in the position of Supreme Chancellor and head of the Republic Senate.

"Your Honor, you cannot allow us to be condemned without reasonable observation. It's against all the rules of procedure...."
—Lott Dod

SUPREME CHANCELLOR VALORUM

As the elected leader of the Senate, Supreme Chancellor Valorum has tried very hard to maintain order and civility in the Galactic Senate. However, with corruption gaining power all around him, he appears ineffectual and weak. When the Trade Federation blockades Naboo, it is Valorum who tries to aid Queen Amidala. After this plan falls through, however, he is betrayed by the Senator from the very planet he was trying to aid and is voted out of office.

Chancellor Valorum tried to help the blockaded planet of Naboo by secretly sending Jedi Qui-Gon Jinn and Obi-Wan Kenobi to negotiate with the Trade Federation.

LIAM NEESON plays Qui-Gon Jinn. He has appeared in over thirty films, but this is the first role to place him inside a spaceship cockpit. "The cockpit scenes, I must admit, were very odd. Every science fiction series flashed into your mind. We'd all look at each other. Doors going, 'Sssshhh,' coming through them being very serious. 'Head for that solar system.' 'No, no. Head for that one.' 'No, head for that one.' Not that these are quotes from the script. It was great fun. That was always the thing I remembered." Neeson has also starred in *Rob Roy*, *Schindler's List*, and *Michael Collins*.

EWAN McGREGOR assumes the role of Obi-Wan Kenobi, the Jedi apprentice to Qui-Gon Jinn. "To be a part of a legend, to be a part of a modern myth, and to play the young Alec Guinness is an incredible honor," McGregor admits. "It's the most exciting thing I've ever known, to have my own lightsaber. I can't have it in my hand and not give it a few twirls." McGregor's other films include *Emma* and *Trainspotting*. On television he has appeared in *ER* and *Tales from the Crypt*. Coincidentally, McGregor is the nephew of Denis Lawson, the actor who played Wedge Antilles in the classic *Star Wars trilogy*.

NATALIE PORTMAN plays the beautiful and resourceful Queen Amidala. Since her screen debut at age twelve in *The Professional*, Portman has also performed in *Heat*, *Beautiful Girls*, *Everyone Says I Love You*, and *Mars Attacks!* "She is a wonderful, serious, deeply committed and focused actress," praises producer Rick McCallum. "She was always our first choice for this role." In 1997, Portman starred on Broadway in *The Diary of Anne Frank*. Raised on the East coast, Portman is an honors student who enjoys writing, dancing, and spending time with her friends.

JAKE LLOYD has performed in over thirty television commercials, and he appeared in the films *Unhook the Stars* and *Jingle All the Way* before getting the call for *The Phantom Menace*. For the nine-year-old Lloyd, the role of Anakin Skywalker was a dream come true. "When I was six, I was Darth Vader for Halloween. Now I get to be a Jedi again!" Almost 3,000 other actors also auditioned for the prized role of Anakin. "I waited two years to get that part," remembers Lloyd. "I auditioned two times." Says Lloyd of playing the role, "He's a lot like me. I love doing mechanics, he is one mechanical kid. I like to build stuff, he likes to build stuff. I just act like myself." Praised for his professionalism and talent by his co-stars, Lloyd says that getting started as an actor was easy: "I just begged." His parents helped him find a manager and an agent, and soon Lloyd found himself in California, where his family had recently moved from Colorado. Filming Episode I was an experience he will never forget. Even the props, costumes, and sets were unlike anything he'd ever seen. "It was just fantastic. I was blown away the first day!"

 **IAN MCDIARMID** originated the role of Palpatine, as the evil Emperor, in *Return of the Jedi*. In that performance, the actor is unrecognizable beneath heavy layers of makeup. Over the years, people have jokingly presented him with Emperor action figures. "Our company manager was in New York, and he brought back a fascinating little one that actually does shoot those thunderbolts," McDiarmid recalls. "When I see it, I think, 'God, I wish I had just a little bit of that in my pinky every now and again. I wouldn't hurt anybody, but it would be nice.'"

 **PERNILLA AUGUST** draws high praise from producer Rick McCallum for her performance as Shmi Skywalker. "She's a lovely and wonderful actress. She has all the dignity and power that you could ever want for the role of Anakin's mother." Winner of the Best Actress Award at the 1992 Cannes Film Festival for her role in *The Best Intentions*, Pernilla August has also appeared in the films *Fanny and Alexander, Tuppen, Jerusalem,* and *Private Confessions*.

 **AHMED BEST** provides the voice and movements of computer-generated Jar Jar Binks. After testing a number of actors, George Lucas realized that the Gungan's voice was "very hard dialogue to understand and make work. Kind of like Yoda times ten. But Ahmed Best just sort of took to it. A lot of people couldn't figure it out. They couldn't equate what they were saying with real life, but he really gets it, and he's turned it into a real language and [Jar Jar into] a real character."

 **SAMUEL L. JACKSON** plays Mace Windu, a senior member of the Jedi Council. His many films include *Pulp Fiction, Die Hard with a Vengeance,* and *Jackie Brown*. Jackson confesses he's always been a big fan of *Star Wars*. "It was everything I had always wanted a film about space to be—you know, guys with lightsabers, really fast-moving planes, the costumes—everything was just right. It was like somebody had stepped into my mind and had taken everything that I wanted to happen and made it happen."

 **RAY PARK** plays Darth Maul. A martial artist and professional stuntman, Park doubled for Rayden in *Mortal Kombat: Annihilation* before landing the role of the fearsome Sith Lord. "People on the set would get scared when I had the lenses in my eyes and the makeup, and my teeth." Park has been a *Star Wars* fan since childhood, when he and his younger brother staged their own lightsaber battles. Now twenty-four, he greatly enjoyed sparring with Liam Neeson and Ewan McGregor in Episode I. "The last fight that Ewan and I did together was really fiery. We both really went for it. He fed off me and I fed off him. The energy we had was really good, and also with Liam."

A PEEK BEHIND THE SCENES

Making a movie requires contributions from many talented people. Sets must be designed and constructed. Costumes are created and tailored. Sound, lighting, visual effects, music score, transportation...the list goes on and on. For George Lucas, one of the great challenges of *Star Wars* is to make fantastic characters and imaginary planets totally believable. Every detail in the film must look right. Lucas notes, "In a film like this, where we're creating a world that doesn't exist, it's very easy to puncture a viewer's sense of reality by a missing or wrong detail."

WHAT DOES A DIRECTOR DO?

A film director attempts to tell a story with moving pictures, transforming a writer's screenplay into a movie. Because George Lucas not only directed but also wrote the screenplay for *The Phantom Menace*, he had a great amount of control in fulfilling his creative vision. To make a film, a director must supervise and instruct actors and a crew on a daily basis. Since so many people can be involved, this is never an easy task.

Just one example of the many challenges faced by Lucas while filming Episode I occurred on July 29, 1997, when a massive storm swept across the edge of the North African Sahara and devastated the Tatooine set. Buildings were destroyed, dressing room tents were torn to ribbons, and droids lay scattered in the rain-drenched sand. Fortunately, no one was injured. According to actor Ewan McGregor, George Lucas was not at all rattled by the sandstorm. "George said, 'Oh, this is a good omen.' And we said, 'What?!' But he said, 'Oh, this happened in the first one, and this is a good thing that we've had our set destroyed.' And everyone just carried on."

Lucas himself defines good directing as getting the best out of cast and crew. "The craft of filmmaking is very difficult, very technical, and very involved," Lucas says. "I become impatient with people who aren't really on top of things. I appreciate professionalism. I feel strongly that it's the absolute foundation of directing."

George Lucas directs actors Liam Neeson and Ewan McGregor. The final glow on the lightsaber props will be added in post-production by the visual effects artists of Industrial Light & Magic.

On Episode I's main hangar set, Director George Lucas (seated) prepares to begin shooting with the 1st unit film crew.

What does a Producer do?

As Rick McCallum says, the job of a film producer "is basically to do everything necessary to make it possible for the director to realize his vision." McCallum was involved in all phases of Episode I's production, from the earliest location scouting to the final stages of visual effects. It was McCallum's job to find the right people for every part of the Episode I production team and to make sure that the team worked effectively together. Managing budgets, complex schedules, and huge numbers of personnel, McCallum served as the marshal for the production army, orchestrating its resources so that it was as responsive as possible to Director George Lucas. McCallum has produced many features for film and television, as well as the restoration and enhancement work done for the *Star Wars* Trilogy Special Edition.

What does a Director of Photography do?

In Europe the position is called cinematographer, but by whatever title, the director of photography is responsible for the vital task of overseeing the camera and lighting crews and helping to create the atmosphere of the film. During principal photography for Episode I, Director of Photography David Tattersall worked closely with George Lucas and the rest of the production crew to shoot the film. He carefully prepared each scene so that everything was ready for when Lucas called, "Action!" Tattersall's challenges included filming in the broiling hot Tunisian desert and shooting against yards of blue screen material at England's Leavesden Studios.

Director of Photography David Tattersall (right) consults with Director George Lucas during filming on the Tunisian set.

Members of the 2nd unit film crew prepare to shoot a Tusken Raider.

WHAT DOES A CONCEPT DESIGNER DO?

As Concept Designer for Episode I, Doug Chiang was responsible for producing paintings that would communicate the visual style of the film. He created the designs for dozens of vehicles, buildings, and weapons. For inspiration, Chiang studied the art of Ralph McQuarrie and Joe Johnston, the concept designers for the previous *Star Wars* films, but he was also encouraged by George Lucas to use his imagination. According to Chiang, "That's when I realized that this was going to be something new and not just a rework of the earlier material."

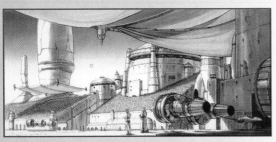

Doug Chiang, Concept Designer.

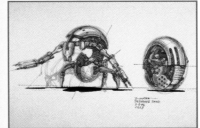

Production Designer Gavin Bocquet consults with George Lucas on the look of an outdoor Naboo set as well as a variety of Episode I props.

WHAT DOES A PRODUCTION DESIGNER DO?

Working from Doug Chiang's elaborate designs, Production Designer Gavin Bocquet was in charge of turning ideas and concept art into three-dimensional sets. "Generally my role is to produce any constructed background that you see behind the actors, whether it's an in-studio set or on location, including props and set dressing."

Trisha Biggar, Costume Designer.

Trisha Biggar consults with George Lucas on the costuming of the Naboo Royal Security Forces.

WHAT DOES A COSTUME DESIGNER DO?

In less than a year, Trisha Biggar created and oversaw production for over one thousand costumes for Episode I. Both human and alien outfits were required, and they all had to fit perfectly. Biggar used concept designs by Iain McCaig, who was inspired by historical costumes from many cultures. "The costumes have all been drawn from the past," notes Biggar. "A long time ago. Not futuristic."

Jar Jar Binks was created through computer-generated technology.

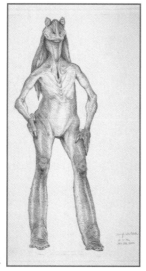

WHAT IS CG TECHNOLOGY?

While making the first *Star Wars* film, George Lucas founded his own visual-effects company and named it Industrial Light & Magic (ILM). Besides the *Star Wars* and *Indiana Jones* films, ILM has created visual effects for a wide range of films, including *Terminator 2: Judgment Day*, *Jurassic Park*, and *Casper*. These motion pictures all employed computer-generated (CG) visual effects.

Before CG technology, movie aliens and monsters usually were portrayed by either an actor in a costume or a stop-motion puppet. Today, creatures can be produced almost entirely on a computer. A significant addition to the *Star Wars* saga is the CG character Jar Jar Binks.

Jar Jar began as a sketch by Iain McCaig. From this sketch, modelers designed a CG version of Jar Jar. To "build" Jar Jar, the modelers created a three-dimensional, wire-frame skeleton of the Gungan. Later, they added moving muscles and skin textures, creating an incredibly realistic picture of Jar Jar.

Actor Ahmed Best provided the voice and mannerisms for Jar Jar Binks. Carefully matching the voice to the computer image, the animators created a walking, talking CG image of Jar Jar, capable of interacting with the human actors on-screen. In each scene, the animators took great care to illuminate Jar Jar in the same light that falls on other characters. The result is so convincing, Jar Jar is able to look at the ground and see his own shadow!

WHAT IS BLUE SCREEN TECHNOLOGY?

To make actors appear to walk on a faraway planet without building an impossibly expensive set, visual effects artists use a production technique called blue screen photography. This technique places actors or objects against a separately filmed background, and can make incredible scenes look absolutely real.

First, actors are photographed in front of an illuminated blue screen. When the film is processed, the actors are isolated from the blue screen background. Afterward, the isolated image of the actors is added to a separately filmed background; this background could be a painting, a photograph, a computer-generated environment, or a combination of all these elements. In the final version, the actors and background are perfectly matched. The blue screen technique can be so convincing that audiences are often unaware they are seeing the result of visual effects.

Blue screen and CG are just two of the many ingenious moviemaking techniques that have allowed audiences to travel back to a time long ago and a galaxy far, far away…

The breathtaking cityscape of Coruscant is actually a digital matte painting that has been added to the Jedi Council chamber scene by way of a visual effects process known as blue screen.